MONSTER PARTY

VISIT
WWW.MONSTERHIGH.COM

This edition published by Parragon Books Ltd in 2013
and distributed by

Parragon Inc.
440 Park Avenue South, 13th Floor
New York, NY 10016
www.parragon.com

ISBN 978-1-4723-2744-4

Printed in China

MONSTER PARTY

Host a party, Monster High™ style!
Find out all the ghouls' party secrets ...
your ghoulfriends will be ugh-mazed.

Contents

Creepy invitations

Here are some drop-dead gorgeous invites for your ugh-mazing monster party. You can trace or copy them, then fill them out and give them to your ghoulfriends. It'll be creepetific!

Lagoona Blue

Bubbly venue:

Monster time: DOSTRNV

Aquatic activities: PAJJ
ᚺᚲᚺ OᚹOᚺᛈ

Dress code: T ᛩ VVᛖ

Clawdeen Wolf

Howlin' venue: Oᚼᛈ᚜ HE
S Oᚹᛈᚺ

Monster time: SAᛈMN

Clawsome activities: MEAN
ᛈOᛖᚼN

Dress code: ᚴ ᛖᚴᛈ

Lagoona Blue™

THE BUBBLIEST HYDRO-PARTY!

Only four days until the most aquatic monster high party ever. I hope Gil comes, he's so sweet!

THE PLAN:

Here's how my party will impress the gods of the oceans....

- It will start at dusk, while the sun is setting over the sea.
- It will be a saltwater party—the only thing sweet will be Gil.
- All the guests will wear blue, the most aquatic color!
- I'll serve seaweed salad.
- There will be starfish masks for the ghouls to wear.
- The boys will wear sea horse masks!
- There will be fins and gills for everybody—no one should miss a swim!
- I'll have vaporizers to keep everyone's scales glossy.
- Gossips and arguments will all be forgotten—water under the bridge!

Not even the Loch Ness Monster could throw a party like this!

Aquatic party favor

I want my party to be remembered for all marine eternity, so I'll give my guests bottles of saltwater with seaweed inside. Fishy and delishy, right?!

legends of the sea

After a good swim, we'll gather by the lake and tell spooky sea-monster stories until our scales dry out in terror. I'll tell a monstrous tale set in Black Lagoon. Cover your fins!

Neptuna

Neptuna will be a freaktacular hostess to all the monster pets!

Monster beach style

Although I'm the hostess, I wouldn't think of giving up my monster-marine comforts. I'll wear my silvery rhinestone T-shirt with an electric blue miniblazer, my marine shorts, and my sequined flip-flops. I'll look like a deep-sea mermaid!

my motto:
Being kind is scary-cool. Be at peace with your fellow monsters.

I don't go out without my vaporizer. When I'm up to my neck in water, a few puffs and my scales are as good as new. I also never forget my coral necklaces and bracelets that my father, the sea monster, gave me.

the venue

After thinking it over for a while, I've decided to have my party at ... Gloom Beach! One of my favorite places is the auditorium there—it fits an ocean of monsters—and the swimming pool.... And there's a fangtastic underwater camp, too! There's no better place to have my party!

Underwater gossip....

Some photos of me and Gil were published in the Monster High Fearbook last year. Since then, there have been so many rumors about us.

JEEPERS CREEPERS!

Every time I'm with him my heart bubbles.

Clawdeen Wolf

A CLAWSOME PARTY!

GRRR! A SHE-WOLF LIKE ME CAN ONLY HAVE THE MOST HAIR-RAISING AND TERRIFYING PARTY OF ALL, BECAUSE ... IT'LL BE A FULL MOON!

THE PLAN:

My party will roOOOaaar because....

- I'll post the invitation on my blog and tag all my ghoulfriends.
- I'll serve up lots of fresh meat for guests to dig their fangs into.
- There'll be huge spotlights, like 20 full moons!
- There will be a stage for wild dancing.
- No slow music—this will be one for party animals!
- The walls will be decorated with animal prints.
- I'll show a video of the Monstermodel Contest highlights!
- My special guest will be ... opera singer Crescenda Von Hammerstone— only her howl is louder than mine!

10

Horrorscope

The most handsome werewolves from Monster High will be coming to my party, and my horrorscope says I'll find my true love! I have to look wildly divine!

Monster Karaoke

All my guests will be able to choose their favorite monster-tune from their iCoffin ... and we'll wail horrifying songs that will scare the daylights out of you!

MONSTER HIGH'S NEXT TOP MONSTER!

At my party, nobody can miss my fashion parade—it'll be wild! I'm planning to win with my final spine-chilling pose.

WILD BEAUTY

My complete beauty session will make my skin glow! Also, I'll file my claws and wear my favorite studded leather collar.

The Song of the Wolf

What better place to have my party than the Howlitorium? Crescenda Von Hammerstone is going to perform "The Song of the Wolf." Isn't that incredible?!

my motto:

Some monsters say I've got an eye for fashion, and I have to admit they're right!

> I have more party spirit in one claw than other monsters have in their whole body.

No competitions!

You all know I love to compete, especially because I always win....

But this time there won't be any races, games, or anything that makes me sweat. I need to look claw-tastic.

Totally wild party favors

Every monster will take home a claw-shaped necklace—on a gold chain, of course! It'll be next season's fashion piece to die for!

MONSTER GUEST

Sometimes I want to throw Cleo and her pharonic platform shoes into the Pit of Horror ... but a party without that ghoul would be like a night without a full moon.

Draculaura

A HORROR-MANTIC PARTY!

So, monsters, it's finally time for my horror-mantic party. If it was up to me, only super-in-love couples would be invited. But I'm going to invite everyone from Monster High, even the zombies!

THE PLAN:

This is how a romantic vegetarian vampire does it....

- I'll send invitations by text, like a piece of juicy gossip!
- There'll be mint chewing gum for everyone, in case they've eaten garlic.
- I'll put red hearts and white candles everywhere.
- No mirrors! What would I need them for? They don't reflect me!
- It'll be a ghostly night and terrifyingly romantic.
- Everyone will have a little heart drawn on their cheek.
- There will be fruit, vegetables, and cereal to eat.
- I'll blog about the party from the first minute until centuries after it ends!
- The photos will go in the Gory Gazette.

This is going to be one of my biggest problems ... how am I going to look deadly divine at my party if I can't see myself in the mirror? I'm going to ask Clawdeen and Frankie for help. It's the only way to make sure I look fangtastic!

Pizza contest!

It's not the coolest thing ever, right? But Clawd loves pizza, and he is so freakily nice. So it's decided—I'll organize a contest to see which monster can eat the most pizzas. Clawd Wolf will win for sure. Then he'll be falling at my platform-shoed feet!

Crazy for Clawd Wolf

It's no secret, ghoulfriends, that a while ago a post about me and Clawd Wolf was published on the Ghostly Gossip blog. But in case you didn't know ... I would lose a fang for that wolf boy! Of course, he'll be the first I'll invite to my party!

Not even ghosts have worn white since pink and black came into fashion!

A place for horror-romance

MY PARTY HAS TO HAPPEN IN A REEEALLY ROMANTIC PLACE. I COULD DECORATE MONSTER HIGH'S GYM WITH WHITE CANDLES AND WHITE CURTAINS THAT FLUTTER IN THE BREEZE ...DOESN'T THAT SOUND SPOOKY?

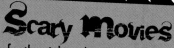Scary Movies

Of course, for the night owls, I'll play Twilight Terror 3. I've already seen it 1001 times, but it's so mortally beautiful! Frankie still hasn't seen it, and I'm sure Clawd won't mind watching it a few more times....

Midnight music

Holt Hyde will play another session of the century! All the monsters will be grooving, and Frankie's sparks are bound to be flying.

Party favor

I'll ask the Ghostly Gossip to take a photo of every couple at the party for them to take home! Unfortunately, Clawd will appear on his own, poor thing. But it'll still be a hair-raising pic!

Draculaura & Clawd

Cleo de Nile ™

♥ A GOLDEN PARTY!

*F*or centuries, I've organized parties for my admirers to come and worship me. Naturally, this is going to be another perfect party.

☠ THE PLAN; ☠

This is how I'll make my party totally golden....

◆ I'll announce my party on the Ghostly Gossip blog.
◆ I'll arrive last and make an unforgettable entrance.
◆ I'll let everyone kiss my solid gold beetle ring.
◆ I'll play the song that Deuce and Operetta wrote about me.
◆ I won't let bad spirits like my sister, Nefera, enter.
◆ All of the guests will get down on their knees to admire my beauty.
◆ As leader of the Fearleading Squad, I'll naturally perform for my guests.
◆ Since it's a party, I *will* let people look me directly in the eyes.
◆ Of course, everything will be perfect—because it's a Cleo de Nile party!

goddess style

Golden beetles hanging from my divine ears, a monstrously fabulous outfit, and some platform sandals that not even my goddess sister Nefera would dream of wearing. I'll dethrone anyone who dares to compete with me on that night.

Cleo de Nile

Party favor for the fortunate

I can't imagine a better souvenir of my party than my own portrait, or maybe a statue . . .

gargoyles to gargoyles

Oh, did you know that this is my favorite game? They say I'm very competitive, but I swear it's not true! The fact is, I'm the best and the only one who deserves to win. There's a reason why they say "Only a de Nile can beat another de Nile". And Nefera isn't going to show her bandages at my party, so my dear monster friends can just applaud my victories.

ultra-tomb mirrors

SO THAT EVERYONE CAN ADMIRE MY AGELESS BEAUTY, I'LL PUT MIRRORS ON EVERY WALL AT MY PARTY. THAT WAY THEY'LL BE ABLE TO CONTEMPLATE MY STUNNING PROFILE FROM ALL ANGLES.

Beauty Queen

*I*n reality, it's not like I have to do anything special to look amazing at my monster party. But I'll perform some beauty rituals anyway. First, I'll have a hot bath in golden calf milk to soften my bandages, then I'll apply some Egyptian honey conditioner so that my long hair is even more spectacular. Finally, I'll put on some ancient amber perfume so that I smell divine.

my motto:
I'm not bossy, I'm entitled, and my party should be perfect!

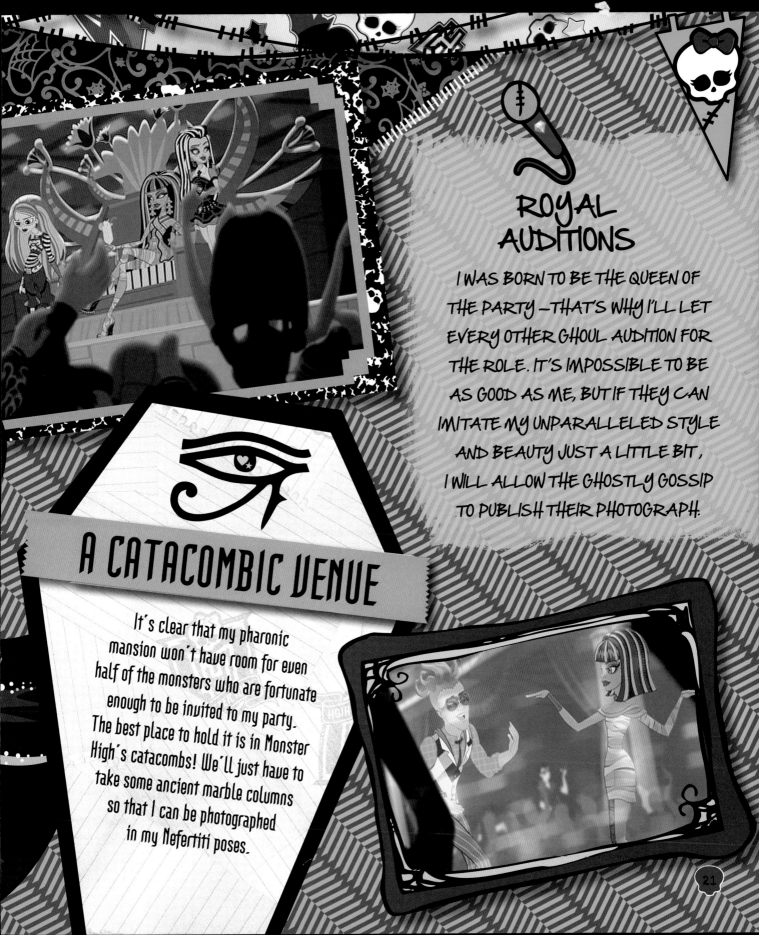

ROYAL AUDITIONS

I WAS BORN TO BE THE QUEEN OF THE PARTY —THAT'S WHY I'LL LET EVERY OTHER GHOUL AUDITION FOR THE ROLE. IT'S IMPOSSIBLE TO BE AS GOOD AS ME, BUT IF THEY CAN IMITATE MY UNPARALLELED STYLE AND BEAUTY JUST A LITTLE BIT, I WILL ALLOW THE GHOSTLY GOSSIP TO PUBLISH THEIR PHOTOGRAPH.

A CATACOMBIC VENUE

It's clear that my pharonic mansion won't have room for even half of the monsters who are fortunate enough to be invited to my party. The best place to hold it is in Monster High's catacombs! We'll just have to take some ancient marble columns so that I can be photographed in my Nefertiti poses.

Ghoulia Yelps

♥ AN UGHSOME ZOMBIE PARTY

I don't like being the center of attention, but I resurrect myself by thinking about the scary-cool time my fellow zombies will have!

💀 THE PLAN: 💀

My mathematical calculations say that....

★ Sir Hoots-a-Lot has failed to deliver the invitations so I'll have to send a group email.
★ I'll need bug zappers so the flies don't annoy the non-zombie monsters.
★ There will be a table of laptops for internet-surfing and computer games.
★ A photo op will immortalize the zombie party.
★ There will be a zombie translator for everybody.
★ Die-hard fans of the Superzombie comic will need some copies to read!

$$f(x) = \frac{1}{3^\sqrt{}}$$

$$\{(a+b=)a|c)$$
$$\{A|3=C\}\infty$$

BFF

ZOMBIE FASHION

For an occasion like this, I'll wear my most shabby formal wear—the Ghost and Gabbana dress given to me by my great-zombie-grandmother, which fits me like a skull. I'll brush my long hair with the brush I found in the scary swamp and use the grayest powder I can find on my skin.

MONSILES (1-1gh)

Warning: slooow party

I'm sure of one thing—my party is going to be the looooooongest one of all. That's why we're going to start first thing in the morning. By the time the sun sets, all of the zombies will have dragged themselves to the party.

A SCARY VENUE....

The ideal place for a zombie party is on the grass behind the school—it's the gloomiest part of Monster High. There, my zombie guests can drag themselves around as much as they like and groan to their hearts' content. The shadows of the graves and the bare trees will make a scary-cool backdrop.

23

MH!

Mad Science

I'll organize some Mad Science exhibits for only the most daring. Curious guests will be able to see dead cells under the monsterscope. There will be transforming rays, zombie-cosmetics ... Mr. Hackington would be impressed!

NecroCon

My parents didn't let me go to the last NecroCon, so I'll create my own convention. At my party there'll be a giant table covered in zombie comics, plus costumes of the most terrifying zombie heroes! And, thanks to Cleo, I can show everybody the issue of *Superzombie: The Elusive Unreachable* that she gave me!

jason biter

What would my ghoulfriends do without music? Cleo's suggestion was the one and only Jason Biter. I'm not in tatters over him, but I am willing to die a thousand times over for my friends. Jason's going to give a spine-chilling performance!

MH!

my motto:
Think fast but move slow

SLO MO

That zombie gets my guts in a whirl! Of course I'm going to invite him to my party, but I'll warn him—no slow-fighting other zombies over me!

Frankie Stein™

A HIGH-VOLTAGE PARTY

I'M GIVING OFF SPARKS COUNTING DOWN THE DAYS UNTIL MY ELECTRIFYING PARTY. I SPARK JUST THINKING ABOUT EVERYTHING I HAVE TO DO!

THE PLAN:

This is how I'm going to make the sparks fly....

⚡ I'll put up a neon sign that says, "Come in and switch on."
⚡ There'll be a Monster News report: Blackout due to oversupply of energy at Frankie's party!
⚡ There will be sparklers and fireworks!
⚡ We'll play "pin the arm on the monster."
⚡ I'll serve up bolt-shaped candy.
⚡ My GFFs from the Fear Squad will light up the dance floor!

Just thinking about my party gets my heart sparking!

At my party, I'll spark brighter than ever before! I'll wear a plaid skirt with a black tank top, a belt with a scary-cool safety pin, and, to finish the outfit, some incredible platform shoes. I'll dazzle all my ghoulfriends!

high-voltage music

HOLT HYDE WILL COME TO MY PARTY AND DO A DJ SESSION, FOR SURE! I CAN FEEL MY BOLTS RATTLING JUST THINKING ABOUT IT. IT'S GOING TO BE ELECTRIFYING!

*I*s there any better place to have my party than the lab in my parents' basement? There's a reason I call it "the fab" you know!! It will be super-original, decorated in freaky-fab black and white, with mirror balls and sparklers—the dance floor will shine brighter than the Milky Way. It will be positively electrifying!

Party preparations

Before the party, I'll have a steam bath to soothe my stitches and leave me super-soft and shiny. Sometimes my high-voltage sparks make my hair frizzy, so I'll use some serum to keep it smooth. I'm going to look freaktastic!

Stitched-up in love

One thing I really need for my party is ... a date! Most of my ghoulfriends already have monster boys, so I made one for myself. Clever, right? His name is HooDude. He just doesn't talk much, and he's made of rags....

Important:
I must record all the monstrous moments with my iCoffin so I can upload them later.

ELECTRIFYING DANCE

My heart still skips a beat when I think about how much dancing we'll do at my party! It will be the perfect place to start planning a new fearleading routine with the ghouls.

29

Which ghoul are you?

COMPLETE THIS SCARY-COOL QUIZ TO FIND OUT WHICH MONSTER HIGH HOSTESS YOU ARE!

1 Which of these parties do you think sounds the most creeptastic?

A The golden party.
B The bubbliest hydro-party.
C The clawsome party.
D The zombie party.
E The horromantic party.
F The high-voltage party.

2 What gift would you like your guests to bring you?

A A crown, because I am party royalty!
B A donation toward saving the whales, because I don't need anything.
C Scary-cool clothes and accessories.
D The new issue of my favorite comic.
E A giant heart-shaped pillow. Soooo romantic!
F I don't care, as long as it's electrifying!

3 What color would you choose for the decorations?

A Gold, of course. Everything will be gold!
B Blue, like the sea.
C Copper.
D Red.
E Pink.
F Black-and-white stripes.

4 If it were a costume party, what would you dress up as?

A Dress up? Me? Not for all the gold in ancient Egypt!
B A sea horse, or anything that lives under the sea.
C A tigress. I'd look wildly stylish!
D A scientist in a white coat. I love discovering things.
E As a vampire who is deeply in love.
F I'd paint my skin mint green and look totally voltage!

5 What food would you serve at your party?

A Let the guests bring the food! The most I'd offer would be some grapes.
B Anything but seafood or fish!
C Spanish omelette, cold cuts of meat, and sausages.
D Snacks that are scientifically proven to be dead-licious.
E Fruit and vegetables for my fangs. Lots of vitamins!
F Freaky-fun munchies—eye candy and sandwiches with extra ketchup.

6 After the party, you would...

A Immediately send everyone a text about how stylish it was!
B Like to know that everyone had a freaky-fab time.
C Hello?! Be the most popular ghoul in school!
D Clean up, then compile a list of things to do better next time.
E Start planning next year's most romantic event!
F Probably have millions of hits on the video sharing site!

Which of these howling hostesses are you...?

MOSTLY As: Cleo de Nile

You are a party queen!

Is your last name de Nile...? There is no ghoul who overshadows you. You can throw a pharoah-fantastic party! The Ghostly Gossip dies for parties like yours.

MOSTLY Bs: Lagoona Blue
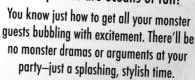

Your parties are oceans of fun!
You know just how to get all your monster guests bubbling with excitement. There'll be no monster dramas or arguments at your party—just a splashing, stylish time.

MOSTLY Cs: Clawdeen Wolf

You're a wickedly wild hostess!
You are the most stylish she-wolf in the pack, and your parties are what all the monsters are howling about. The results are in: you're clawsome!

MOSTLY Ds: Ghoulia Yelps

The hostess with the mostest ... brains!

Your mathematical calculations make all your zombie parties scarlylicious. No-one can mess with you because, whatever happens, you'll always be yourself.

MOSTLY Es: Draculaura
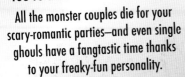

You're a horror-mantic hostess!
All the monster couples die for your scary-romantic parties—and even single ghouls have a fangtastic time thanks to your freaky-fun personality.

MOSTLY Fs: Frankie Stein

You are an electrifying hostess!
Sparks fly at your parties. You wear scary-cute clothes and all your monster guests are guaranteed a high-voltage time. Just don't drain your batteries!

HALLOWEEN

At Monster High, we host the most fangtastic Halloween parties, with spooktacular decorations, fierce fashion, electrifying dancing ... even the headless headmistress comes along!

Petrifying Pumpkins

We always carve bolt-loads of pumpkins for Halloween.
Personally, I'd prefer them to be electrified,
but as long as they have scary-cool faces, I love them!
Sometimes I imagine adding some screws and sparks
and bringing them to life!

Monster idea:

Instead of carving out a pumpkin's insides,
you can simply paint a face with black paint.
Or you can use orange balloons with faces on
them to decorate your fangtastic party!

Trick or treat

Without a doubt, I'll always go
for "treat." Just thinking about
what the monsters from school could
do to me if I chose "trick" sends
chills down my spine. When I meet
the gang of trick-or-treating
zombies in the school halls, I'll fill
their pockets with candy before
they can groan a word.

Clawdeen X

*S*cary-cool costumes are essential at Monster High parties! Will you dress up as Draculaura, Ghoulia, Frankie, or one of the other student bodies?
You can be wildly stylish and spooktactular—just look at the Monster High ghouls!

monster make up

YOUR MAKE UP MUST BE SPINE-CHILLINGLY CLAWSOME! SLAP ON A LAYER OF WHITE POWDER SO THAT YOU LOOK DEATHLY COOL. YOU CAN ALSO ADD FAKE STITCHES, SCARS, AND BLOOD!

A ghostly appearance

You can draw a skeleton on black fabric with white fabric pens, make yourself a plastic scythe, and, if you dare, go as the Grim Reaper! The zombies will give you lots of tips on how to look like the living dead, but if you really want to electrify everyone, don't forget my look: screws, scars, seams, and each eye a different color.

Party at gloom beach™

Be safe!

There's nothing cooler than a party on the beach. You can hold it at a swimming pool, too, but make sure there are always adults around.

- Hang chains of blue baubles everywhere—like bubbles!

- Ask your ghoulfriends to wear a swimsuit with a beach wrap. They'll look swimtastic!

- Make scary-cool shell necklaces for all your monster guests.

- Use a dark blue tablecloth so that your party food looks like it's floating on the ocean.

- Play bubbly-fresh music that makes every monster think of summer.

Wild full-moon party

This is my party, ghoulfriends! I'm going to howl it out loud: whenever there's a full moon there should be a wild party! It doesn't matter if you hold it indoors, I'm going to give you some lunar ideas so your party can shine brighter than 20 full moons.

A PARTY TO HOWL ABOUT....

Animal-print plates, cups, and napkins.

Fake cobwebs sprayed with gold, hanging from the chairs.

Purple and black balloons.

Gold candelabras with purple candles!

A lunar look

Wear a necklace with a big, round pendant. Find long earrings with mirrored metal and paint your nails gold!

A STYLISH TOUCH

Wear glittery eye shadow, dangerously shiny lip gloss, and glitter in your hair. If you want to go even more edgy, use gold body paint to add the shape of a full moon to your cheek. It's wild style!

Scary-cool birthday party

The most monstrous party of all is finally here! You are the center of attention ... it's our birthday ghoul party!

MONSTER IDEA

Make a piñata in the shape of a skullette—you can fill it with candy eyes, bones, and hearts ... your ghoulfriends will think it's clawsome!

Birthday party tips from the ghouls:

- **Draculaura:** Invite all your ghoulfriends—don't forget anyone!

- **Clawdeen:** Send some wildly cool invites with all the party info. Give them something to howl about!

- **Cleo:** Since you're the queen of the party, you should choose a worthy outfit

- **Frankie:** Hang strings of electric lights in the windows!

- **Ghoulia:** Upload a video of the best moments for everyone to see

- **Lagoona:** If there's a monster like Gil in your life, make sure you invite him!

37

Get the party started

*I*f you want your Monster High party to be totally creeptastic, there are preparations to be made! Here are some freaky-fab tips to make it all less terrifying....

better than Gloom Beach!

Decide on a high-voltage venue! You could have your party outside, in a hall or at home. Figure out how many monsters will be coming ... will they all fit? Will it be easy for your guests to get home? If the answers are YES and YES, your venue sounds more fangtastic than Gloom Beach!

Fishing for permission

So now you know where you want to hold your party, but you have to get permission from your parents. Will Mom and Dad let you hold the party? Tell them that you'll do it all: organize, decorate and—the thing that's bound to convince them—clean up afterwards. I'm sure they'll agree!

SPOOKTACULAR SCHEDULE

The party shouldn't run too late or start too early—all the ghouls need time to make themselves gore-geous. Always put the start and end time on the invite, so your guests can plan.

getting home

It might be the case that some monster parent can't pick up their ghoul after the party, or that they live megawatts away. Don't let it give you an electric shock! Maybe your own creators can take your ghoulfriend home? Or maybe she can sleep over? Voltage!

Ask your GFFs....

You don't want to end up coming apart at the seams planning everything for your party. So don't be scared to ask for help! Your GFFs can help you make the freaky-fab decorations, and you can always ask guests to bring snacks or their favorite bottle of soda with them!

Vamp-tastic snacks

Vegetarian burgers!

My fangs water when I think about this delicious snack. It's to die for! Making these is easier than putting on lipstick when you have no reflection.

TO MAKE ONE BURGER:

- 1 vegetarian soy or bean burger
- 2 pieces of thick bread
- A few leaves of lettuce
- 2 slices of fresh tomato
- Ketchup

Top tip: Cut the bread and burger into heart shapes, then dribble some creeptastic ketchup shapes on top.

40

bolts!

YOU'LL NEED:

- Thick slices of salami
- Cheddar cheese
- Skewers (wooden or plastic)
- Cherry tomatoes
- Olives

Frankie's tip:

TO AVOID ANY VOLTAGEOUS FAILS, ASK AN ADULT TO HELP YOU!

To make one Bolt:

- Carefully cut the slices of salami into little lightning bolt shapes.
- Cut the cheddar cheese into fun shapes using a cookie cutter or knife—you could make circles and squares to look like bolts.
- Take a skewer and thread a lightning bolt, a cherry tomato, a piece of cheese, an olive, then a second lightning bolt onto it.
- Make enough Bolts to electrify everybody's taste buds!

Coffin sandwiches

These sandwiches are fit for ancient royalty, so get to work!

FOR YOUR COFFINS:

- Sliced bread
- Cold roast beef, cut into thin slices
- Ketchup

With a plastic knife, cut the slices of bread into coffin shapes. Place a layer of roast beef on the bottom slice, then dribble with ketchup and cover with the top slice. You can use toothpicks to hold the coffins together.

Cleo's tip:

Cover a tray with golden wrapping paper and serve your coffins on it. Place some glittering decorations in the center and all of your monster guests will fall at your divine feet!

Swamp Fondue

Try this scarylicious dessert! Lagoona may be from the sea, but she knows this recipe from the swamps is a ripper!

INGREDIENTS:

- 1 packet of drinking chocolate
- Fruit (apples, bananas, oranges, strawberries)
- Raspberry jelly or melted chocolate
- Sprinkles or sugar crystals
- Wooden sticks
- Shiny streamers to decorate

Prepare the drinking chocolate. When it's ready, pour it into a wide, shallow container. Draw eyes and scars on the fruit using a stick dipped in raspberry jelly or melted chocolate. Decorate the top of the fondue with the sprinkles or sugar crystals to give it scary-cool Monster High style. Your guests can dip the freaky-fab fruit in the fondue and be ugh-mazed.

LAGOONA'S TIP:

DECORATE THE WOODEN FONDUE STICKS WITH STREAMERS AND COLORED PAPER SHAPES. IT'LL BE A RIPPER OF A PARTY!

42

Scarylicious refreshments

LEMONADE OF THE GODS

Egyptian gods have been drinking this golden lemonade for centuries. It's so freakily fab, it makes my bandages unravel!

How to make it:

Mix together the juice and soda. Pour into a glass and add a scoop of lemon sorbet.

Ingredients:

- 1 cup apple juice
- 1 cup lemon-lime soda
- 1 scoop lemon sorbet
(makes 1 glass)

To decorate:

Use tall glasses and golden straws. Pharaonic!

Hint:

If you prefer, you can use any flavor of soda instead of lemon-lime. Try cherry or tropical!

Nefera has been waiting an eternity to get her hands on this lemonade recipe, but I'll never give it to her!

Only one de Nile is dignified enough for this golden drink.

HORROR-MANTIC JUICE

If you want to ugh-maze your friends with a fangtastically delicious drink, try my horror-mantic juice!

Ingredients

- 8 crushed ice cubes
- 2 tablespoons orange juice
- 2 tablespoons pineapple juice
- 2 tablespoons grapefruit juice
- 2 tablespoons lemon-lime soda
- 2 large splashes of grenadine (makes 1 glass)

Hint:

To crush the ice, place the cubes in a cloth and tie it up well. Then, use something hard (like a rolling pin) to carefully crush the ice into bits. Ask an adult to help you!

How to make it:

- Place half of the crushed ice in a cocktail shaker or a tall glass with a lid. Add the fruit juices, soda, and grenadine.
- Shake well for 1 minute.
- Pour the contents into a wide-rimmed glass.
- Add the remaining crushed ice to the glass.

To decorate:

Put some chocolate sprinkles onto a plate. Dampen the edge of the glass that you're going to serve the juice in, then press it upside down into the choclate. The chocolate will stick to the rim of the glass!

A PARTY ISN'T TRULY WILD WITHOUT A CLAWSOME BEVERAGE. IF YOU DARE, MAKE THIS DRINK FOR YOUR MONSTER GUESTS. THEY ARE GUARANTEED TO HOWL FOR MORE!

Ingredients:

- 4¼ cups red grape juice
- 3¼ cups orange juice
- Juice of 1 lemon
- 2 cinnamon sticks
- Half an apple, diced (makes 6 glasses)

How to make it:

Place all the ingredients in a large jug and mix well. Leave the mixture to settle for 24 hours in the refrigerator. To serve, remove the cinnamon sticks and pour into glasses.

Monster High touch:

You can cut the apple in the shapes of skulls and bones for a totally wild look! Ask an adult to help you.

ZOMBIE ZEST

Zombies love this zesty refreshment—it's good enough to die twice for!

How to make it:

Mix together the crushed ice and mint, and pour into a wide-rimmed glass. Separately, mix the soda with the peach syrup, and then pour into the glass over the the mint and ice. Decorate with mint leaves.

Ingredients:

- 4 crushed ice cubes
- 4–5 mint leaves (crushed), plus extra to decorate
- 1 ¼ cups of lemon-lime soda
- 2 tablespoons of syrup from a can of peaches
(makes 1 glass)

Hint:

Add slices of peach to the drink, too—zombies love them!

THIS COCKTAIL
TASTES BEST WHEN SIPPED
WITH A FUN STRAW!

Party-planning essentials

If you want your party to be as scary-cool as one of mine, remember to plan these simple things—atmosphere, decorations, music, dancing, and, most importantly, outfit!

Atmosphere

For a terrifying atmosphere, remember: dim lights, floaty curtains in the windows, sinister touches such as skulls, and ... use black, everywhere!

Decorations

Hang fake cobwebs from the tables and chairs, stick gold wrapping paper on the wall in the shape of Egyptian columns, wrap the dishes you're going to serve snacks on with gold paper, and, most deadly of all, draw Egyptian symbols on the cups using a gold felt-tip pen.

DEADLY DANCING

Your monster dancing has to be electric! No dragging your platform shoes as if you just got out of your tomb. If you're the ghoully hostess with the mostest, you have to set the pace.

Music

From the very first howl, the atmosphere has to be terror-ific. No zombie groaning allowed ... only electrifying rhythms, clawsome dances, and monstrous howls to the rhythm of the DJ. Of course, you'll need a dance floor fit for the Fearleading Squad themselves.

Outfit

Turn the page to unearth more scary-cool tips on looking as stylish as the Monster High ghouls....

Monster High styles

There's no way you're going plain to a monster party—you want to look totally individual and scarily stylish like the Monster High ghouls!

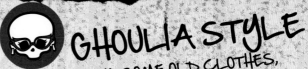

GHOULIA STYLE

TEAR UP SOME OLD CLOTHES, PUT WHITE POWDER ON YOUR FACE, WEAR BLACK EYELINER, AND MAKE FAKE WOUNDS WITH RED LIPSTICK!

golden style

If you want to look perfect and divine, you should wear all the gold accessories you can find. You'll look like a golden goddess!

Golden style

Ghoulia style

Wild style

50

Draculaura style

Does someone have a tie they no longer want? Wear it in a bow like Draculaura's necktie. Also, find tights with love hearts on them!

Beach style

Find some old beach shorts, sew sequins on your flip-flops, and wear lots of scary-cool seashell necklaces!

Wild style

If you really want to make your mark, wear an oversized animal print T-shirt with black tights. Give yourself a wild hairdo using lots of glitter hair spray. To die for!

ELECTRIFYING STYLE

To look as high-voltage as Frankie, wear plaid patterns and lots of chunky silver jewelry. You'll look totally voltage!

Electrifying style

Beach style

Draculaura style

Ghoulish games

FREAKY-FAB SECRETS

Take a standard deck of cards and remove all of the face cards. Shuffle the deck and place it in the middle of the playing area. Players take turns to choose a card and reveal the amount of secrets equal to the number on the card. It'll be creeperific!

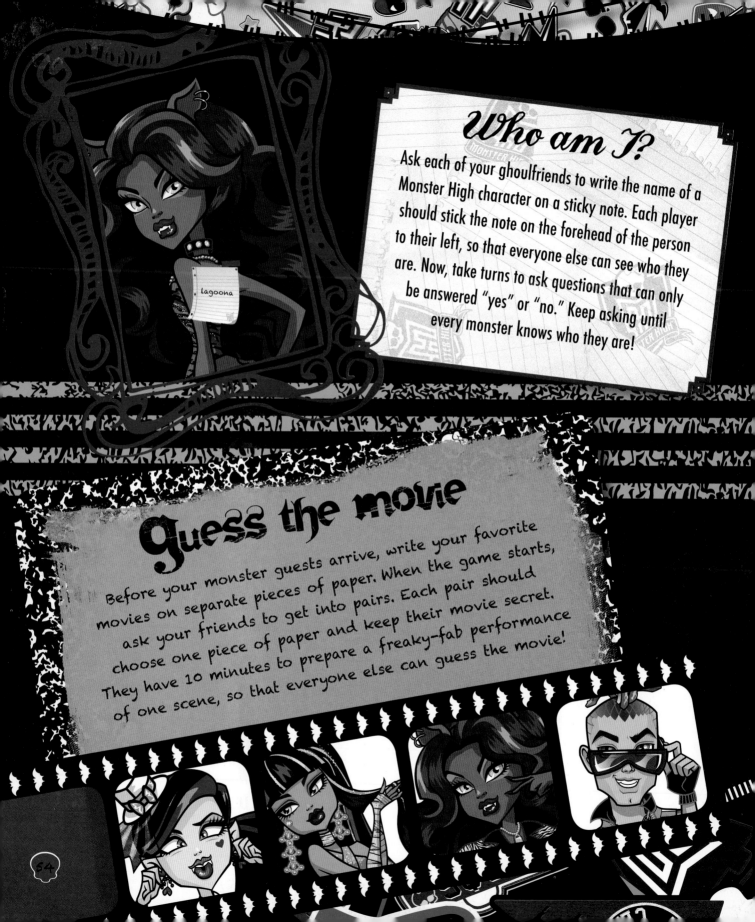

Who am I?

Ask each of your ghoulfriends to write the name of a Monster High character on a sticky note. Each player should stick the note on the forehead of the person to their left, so that everyone else can see who they are. Now, take turns to ask questions that can only be answered "yes" or "no." Keep asking until every monster knows who they are!

lagoona

Guess the movie

Before your monster guests arrive, write your favorite movies on separate pieces of paper. When the game starts, ask your friends to get into pairs. Each pair should choose one piece of paper and keep their movie secret. They have 10 minutes to prepare a freaky-fab performance of one scene, so that everyone else can guess the movie!

Musical runway

Turn your hallway or a corridor into a runway! Put some music on and press stop when you feel like it. When the music plays, your guests should sashay down the catwalk as if they were top monster models, then stop still like Deuce has turned you to stone when the music stops. Anyone who moves is out! The winner is the last monster still in.

Ghoulfriends forever

No monster likes to feel left out or shy at a party, so follow these spookily simple tips for making all your ghoul and guy friends feel fangtastic!

ELECTRIFYING GUEST LIST

Your best ghoulfriends will obviously be first on the list. But don't forget to invite other monsters too—they might be your future best friends!

TO INVITE:
Draculaura
Clawdeen Wolf
Lagoona Blue
Cleo de Nile
Ghoulia Yelps
~~Toralei Stripe~~
Holt Hyde

All kinds of ghouls

THERE ARE THREE IMPORTANT WORDS TO REMEMBER: **THINK OF EVERYONE.**

IF SOMEBODY WHO LIVES IN WATER, LIKES THE COLD, OR IS AFRAID OF THE DARK IS COMING TO YOUR PARTY, MAKE SURE THEY CAN FEEL RIGHT AT HOME AND JOIN IN ALL THE FUN!

Ghoulish GOODBYES

Maybe a monster guest needs to leave before the party is finished? Make sure you say goodbye in true monster fashion. Remember to give them a scary-cool party favor and, the next day, fill them in on all the ghoulish gossip they missed!

Take care of the late monsters!

If you know any guests are going to arrive late, like the slow-moving zombies, don't let the other guys and ghouls eat everything! Put aside some snacks and a fangtastic drink for them.

And when they arrive, play a new game so that they feel part of the freaky fun!

Bye Bye

Bye Bye

Bye Bye

Monster High Quiz

*N*o monster party is complete without a creepy quiz! Test your guests with these Monster High questions. The winner won't be the one that roars or howls the loudest, but the one who whimpers the most answers correctly!

1 WHO IS CLEO DE NILE'S LONG-SERVING BOYFRIEND?

2 WHAT DOES MR. HACKINGTON TEACH?

3 WHAT MONSTER LOVES TO PLAY (AND ALWAYS WINS) THE GAME GARGOYLES TO GARGOYLES?

4 WHAT'S THE NAME OF DEUCE'S TWO-TAILED RAT?

5 WHERE ARE THE COMPETITORS WHO WON THE FEARLEADING FINALS THE LAST FOUR YEARS IN A ROW FROM?

6 WHO LURCHES SLOWLY AROUND MONSTER HIGH AND IS ALWAYS WILLING TO HELP?

7 WHAT'S THE NAME OF HEADMISTRESS BLOODGOOD'S HORSE?

8 WHO KNOWS ALL OF MONSTER HIGH'S GOSSIP AND KEEPS EVERYBODY UP TO DATE?

9 WHAT'S THE CURE FOR A MONSTER HIGH COLD?

10 WHO BROUGHT JASON BITER TO THE SCHOOL?

11 WHAT EFFECT DOES THE EYEBALL CANDY FROM THE MONSTER HIGH VENDING MACHINE HAVE?

12 WHO'S IN CHARGE OF THE AUDITIONS AND THE THEATER AT MONSTER HIGH?

WHO WAS THE MONSTER WITH THE MOST CORRECT ANSWERS? THEY'RE THE WINNER!

ANSWERS:
1. DEUCE GORGON, 2. MAD SCIENCE
3. CLEO DE NILE, 4. PERSEUS
5. SMOGSNORTS VAMPYR ACADEMY, 6. GHOULIA YELPS
7. NIGHTMARE, 8. THE GHOSTLY GOSSIP
9. MONSTER THISTLE, 10. FRANKIE STEIN'S DAD
11. THEY GIVE YOU PIMPLES, 12. MR. WHERE

Ughsome awards!

To make your party totally fangtastic, organize awards to give your guests, and let all the ghouls and guys vote. It'll be freaky-fab fun!

Clawsome idea: Buy some wide strips of ribbon to make winners' sashes! Write an award title on each sash and place it over the shoulder of the winner!

Ghostly gossip award

FOR THE GHOUL THAT TELLS THE MOST ELECTRIFYING AMOUNT OF GOSSIP!

Most spooktacular singer award

For the monster with the best howl at the party!

Cleo de Nile award

FOR THE MOST GHOULISHLY GLAMOROUS DIVA (THE ONE WHO IS MOST LIKE CLEO). IF SHE'S BEEN PHARONICALLY FABULOUS, SHE DESERVES A GOLDEN AWARD!

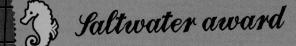

Saltwater award

For the ghoul that helped out the most, just like Lagoona would!

Horror-mantic award

FOR THE MOST ROMANTIC MONSTER COUPLE! THEY'LL BE HOLDING CLAWS FOR ETERNITY.

Terrifying talker award

For the monster who has talked the most at the party!

Fashionista award

For the ghoul with the most fur-rociously fierce outfit and killer style!

Voltageous moves award

For the ghoul with the most groove. Her dancing is electrifying!

Your party will be colossal! And, who knows, maybe you'll receive the award for Best Hostess.... It'll be wild!

Make this clawsome photo album to help you remember your monster party for all eternity! Your scales will shimmer just looking at it!

How to make your creeperific album:

1. Fold the 3 pieces of card stock in half longways.

2. Unfold the pieces of card stock and place them on top of each other.

3. Fold them again, together like a book, and staple along the crease.

4. Think of a title for your photo album and write it on the front cover, then draw a picture or glue a photograph of your party.

5. Open the photo album and write "Monster Messages" at the top of the first two pages. Ask your monster guests to write messages about your party and sign their names underneath.

6. On the rest of the pages you can glue in photographs or souvenirs—perhaps the party invitation or some wrapping paper that will remind you of the fangtastic time you had!

YOU WILL NEED:

- 3 pieces of 11"x17" card stock
- Staples
- Felt-tip pens
- Glue

Cleo's creeperific photo album

An ageless souvenir to keep in your tomb. When you look back at it with your ghoulfriends, it'll bring it all back to life!

$E=mc^2$